A Run of Force and Motion

Dear Reader

When I met David Simon, he told me how he and his brother Mark raced in an ultra-marathon in the Sahara Desert. It was not the usual marathon of 42 kilometres – this one was a 245-kilometre marathon in one of the hottest places on Earth!

> "TWO BROTHERS RACED IN A 245-KILOMETRE MARATHON IN THE SAHARA DESERT."

It was such an amazing story that I wanted to write about it! David and his brother Mark finished the race successfully but they lost many toenails and raced with lots of painful blisters on their backs and their feet.

I hope you enjoy finding out how marathon runners and sportspeople work with forces such as motion, gravity and friction when they want to perform at their best.

Sharon Parsons

My sincere thanks to the following people for their time, information, images and enthusiasm for this book:

David and Mark Simon,
Room to Read charity.

NELSON
CENGAGE Learning™
For learning solutions, visit cengage.com.au

Contents

A RUN OF Force and Motion

1 Force and Motion in Sports

Forces in **Soccer** and **Surfing**

If we apply enough **force** to something, we set it in motion.

Once something is pushed, it will keep moving until something else stops it. **Gravity** and **friction** are forces that can stop the moving object.

FORCE

Force is the energy used to push or pull an object. For example, if an object is heavy and moving fast, more force is needed to slow it down.

FRICTION

The rubbing of one thing against another.

GRAVITY

Gravity is the force that pulls all objects together in the universe. Large masses, like a planet, have stronger gravity than small masses, like a ball.

Forces in Soccer

1 The kick is a **force**.

2 The **force** pushes the ball up.

3 and 4 There is **friction** between the ball and the air, which slows it down.

5 **Gravity** pulls the ball towards Earth.

Forces in Surfing

FRICTION
There is friction between the water and the surfer's hand and board.

GRAVITY
Gravity pulls the surfer down the wave.

FORCE
The force of the waves make the surfboard move.

Skills in Surfing

BUOYANCY
The board floats because of the upward force of the water under the surfboard, which is less dense than the water.

BALANCE
A surfer needs good balance to surf waves.

2 Force and Motion in a Marathon

Meet Two **Brothers**

David and Mark at the ultra-marathon in the Sahara Desert.

In 2008, David and Mark Simon became ultra-marathon runners. They used their own energy and force to run the 245-kilometre *Marathon des Sables*. This is a six-day footrace in one of the hottest places on Earth, the Sahara Desert.

Like most marathon runners, David and Mark have slender bodies. This means they need less energy to move their bodies than heavier people.

Sport and Social Studies

The World's Toughest Footrace

The Marathon des Sables is the toughest footrace in the world. It is run:

- *over a long distance – 245 kilometres in six days (plus one day for rest)*
- *in a hot climate – during the day, it can be between 45 and 50 degrees Celsius*
- *in a harsh environment – over sand dunes, rocky ground, low mountain ranges and salt flats*
- *with a heavy backpack – runners carry a 12-kilogram backpack containing food, water, clothes, a sleeping bag and a first-aid kit.*

the Marathon des Sables

AFTER RUNNING THE *MARATHON DES SABLES* OVER SIX DAYS, THE SIMON BROTHERS ARE NOW CALLED "ULTRA-MARATHON RUNNERS".

Stored Energy

When the Simon brothers trained for the marathon, they ate healthy food. It contained:

- carbohydrates for energy
- fats for energy
- protein for muscle movement.

The food gave them potential energy, which they could use in the marathon.

STORED ENERGY

In science, another term for stored energy is **potential energy**.

History

Marathon des Sables

"Marathon des Sables" is French for "Marathon of the Sands". A Frenchman, Patrick Bauer, had the idea when he walked for 200 kilometres across the Sahara Desert. He wanted other people to enjoy the same experience. Since it began in 1986, over 6000 people have entered the race. Their ages range from 18 to 78.

A Training Program for the *Marathon des Sables*

After Christmas dinner in 2006, David and Mark planned their training program. It would start in February 2007. This was their plan. The *Marathon des Sables* would be their biggest challenge ever!

MONTH 10

Run longer distances with a 9 kg backpack.

MONTH 11

Run longer distances with a 10 kg backpack.

MONTH 12

Run longer distances with an 11 kg backpack.

Run in the Australian desert from Connellan Airport to Uluru and back = 30 kilometres.

Run halfway from Uluru to Kata Tjuta in the desert = 50 kilometres.

MONTH 13

Run longer distances with a 12 kg backpack.

MONTH 14

Run even longer distances with a 12 kg backpack.

SEVEN DAYS BEFORE THE RACE

Travel to Morocco to get used to the hot climate.

SIX DAYS BEFORE THE RACE

Three-day hike up the Atlas Mountains in south-west Morocco.

Climb to the highest mountain peak in the Atlas Mountains – 4165 metres high!

THE RACE IN MARCH 2008

Run the 245-kilometre race with a 12 kg backpack.

3 Force Needs Food

TEXT TYPE
Information Report

Fuel for the Marathon

The *Marathon des Sables* is a very difficult event. The organisers and doctors have strict rules to keep the runners healthy and safe. Some of those rules are about eating, drinking and resting. The runners must be careful to look after themselves by:

David and Mark Simon in their tent at the Marathon des Sables.

- getting their bodies ready for the marathon
- having enough fuel to race throughout the marathon
- helping their bodies recover at the end of each day and at the end of the marathon.

CARBOHYDRATES

Preparing for the Ultra-Marathon

For three days before the marathon, it is important that the runners eat foods containing carbohydrates, such as rice and pasta. Carbohydrates provide energy.

It is also important to drink enough water. Sweating causes water loss during the race. Runners need to drink water before, during and after the race to keep hydrated. But they should not drink too much water while running as this can cause health problems.

WATER

FUEL

ENERGY

Fuel for the Ultra-Marathon

Every morning while the race is on, doctors check the runners' backpacks. Each runner must carry about 2000 calories of food. David and Mark chose food that weighed about 500 grams in total. They packed high-energy food, such as:

- porridge
- dried fruit
- nuts
- fruit cake
- jelly beans
- olive oil.

Eat Food in Thirds

Daily Intake Before the Race

The brothers ate one-third of their food. This intake was mainly carbohydrates.

Daily Intake During the Race

The brothers ate one-third of their food. This intake was mostly small, regular snacks.

Daily Intake After the Race

The brothers ate one-third of their food. This intake mainly consisted of fats and protein.

RECOVER

ENERGY

MOTION

Water

Each day runners are given a water ration. It is between eight and twelve litres. Runners can refill their water bottles every ten kilometres at checkpoints.

Salt Tablets

Runners can lose a lot of salt through their sweat during a marathon. All marathon runners must add salt to their diet every day by:

- taking salt tablets
- adding salt to their food
- drinking sports drinks with salt added.

Without enough salt, runners could:

- get muscle cramps
- lose energy.

Social Studies

Respect for the Desert

Every runner's race number is printed on their water bottle and lid. If they leave their bottle in the desert, the race organisers will find it. As a penalty, they add an hour to the runner's race time. No runner wants that!

At the End of Each Day

At the end of each race day the runners are exhausted. They refuel by eating, drinking and resting. David and Mark got plenty of sleep each night to restore their energy.

FOOD

End of the Marathon

At the end of the marathon, the race organisers give every runner a lunch pack. The food is protein-rich to repair their muscles. Each pack has:

- a sliced meat roll
- cheese
- nuts
- salami
- a can of tuna
- orange juice.

Health

Finally to Bed!

After seven days in the Sahara Desert with no beds and no showers, David and Mark enjoyed their hotel. They also ate a lot of meat, vegetables and fruit.

HYDRATE

A Marathon Effort

The ultra-marathon runners need enough energy to keep running in the hard and hot desert conditions. Their energy helps them with their force and motion.

When marathon runners eat the right food and drink the right drinks, they can run well. This helps keep them healthy before the race, during the race and after the race.

The organisers and doctors are happy when the runners finish the ultra-marathon in a healthy condition.

4 Race Week

Racing in the **Hot Sahara** Desert

The *Marathon des Sables* is run over seven days, with one rest day in the middle. But many runners can't finish their 75.5 kilometre race on day four so they have to run during the fourth night and use their rest day to catch up.

The Race Day-by-Day

Day 1: Race for **31.6 km**

Day 2: Race for **38 km**

Day 3: Race for **40.5 km**

Day 4 (longest day): Race for **75.5 km**

Day 5: Rest day

Day 6: Race for **42.2 km**

Day 7: Race for **17.5 km**

Total: 245.3 kilometres

The Race Road Book

At the start of each day, runners check their road race book. It includes:

- a sketched map of the route for that day's race
- a description of the countryside at each stage of the race
- compass bearings so the runners won't get lost, e.g. NW (North West).

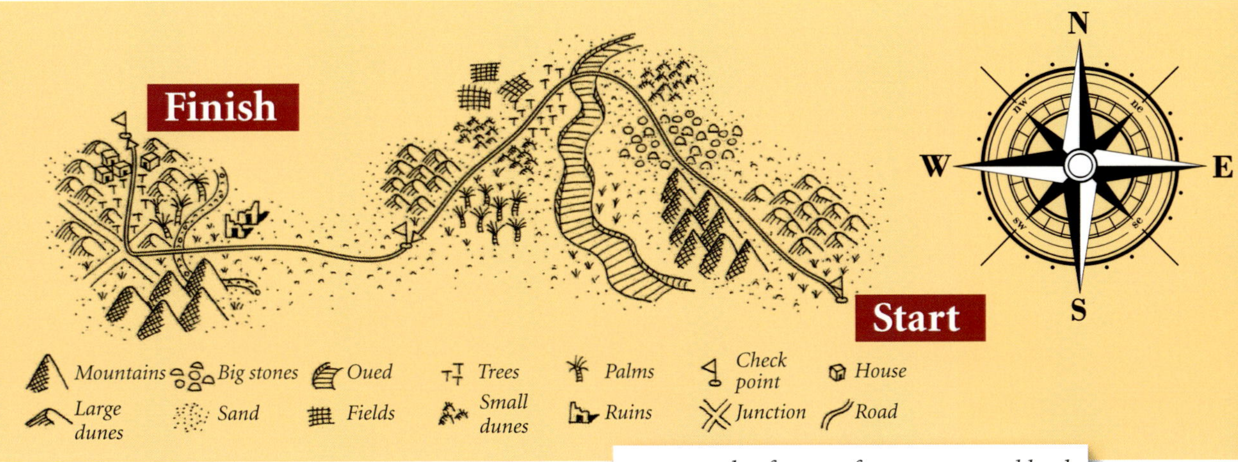

an example of a page from a race road book

Instructions for 17.5 km

Here is an example of some instructions given to runners for a 17.5 km race.

Km 0: Start going NW until you reach the end of the track at **km 8.0**.

Km 1.5: Mountains on left. Large sand dunes on right.

Km 3.5: End of mountains on left. Big stones and sand.

Km 5.0: Pass small dunes on right. Stay NW direction.

Km 6.0: Cross oued.

Km 7.0: Leave oued. Fields on right. Go up hilly track.

Km 8.0: End of track. Go west. Small dunes both sides.

Km 9.0: Pass palm trees on left and large dunes on right. Stay south-west.

Km 10.5: CP1 (check point 1)as you leave dunes. Go west until **km 14.5**.

Km 13.5: Ruins of mining village on right.

Km 14.5: Cross stony track. Palm-trees on right. Mountains on left.

Km 15.5: Go right at junction to track at foot of hill and large dunes.

Km 16.5: Go into village of Tazarine.

Km 17.5: End of dunes. Finish line.

OUED

An oued is a valley or dry riverbed.

Runners Plan Their Run

Each day David and Mark studied the race road book. They saw that some parts of the run were:

- easier during cooler times of the day
- harder during the hottest times of the day
- uphill.

The brothers worked out when to use:

- less force for the easier parts
- more force for the harder parts.

runners' footprints in the desert

A runner is greeted by a local Moroccan girl.

Powerful Sandstorms

The force of strong winds blows millions of grains of sand around. This causes powerful sandstorms.

In the Sahara Desert, the runners have to use more energy to run against the strong forces of the wind and the sand.

People use face masks to protect themselves from sandstorms.

Runners Save Energy

The hills and sand dunes in the Sahara Desert are so steep that the brothers saved their energy by walking up them. If David and Mark had run up the hills and sand dunes, they would have used too much energy and may not have had enough energy left for the race.

Walked Up the Steep Hills

Ran Down the Sand Dunes

5 Running with Force and Friction

Is Friction **Good** or **Bad?**

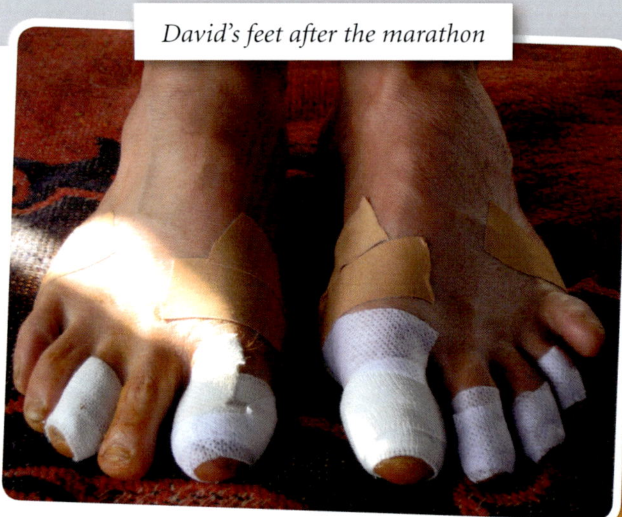
David's feet after the marathon

Friction is a force that can slow or stop something that is moving.

When Friction Is Good

Friction can be good if you are running down a steep footpath. The friction between the soles of your shoes and the surface of the footpath stops you from slipping or falling.

When Friction Is Not Good

Friction isn't good if you're running in shoes that are too loose. The friction between your feet and your shoes can cause pain and blisters!

Friction Is a Runner's Enemy

During the 245-kilometre race, friction was David's enemy. David's worst friction points were his toes, shoulders and back.

Socks, Shoes and Friction

The friction of the socks and shoes rubbing against David's feet caused painful blisters.

FIVE KILOMETRES OF PLASTERS!

Over the six running days of the marathon, doctors used five kilometres of elastoplast to tend to the runners' injuries!

A Backpack and Friction

The friction from David's backpack rubbing against his shoulders and back caused him to have red, sore skin and blisters. They had to be treated and taped by David and the doctors.

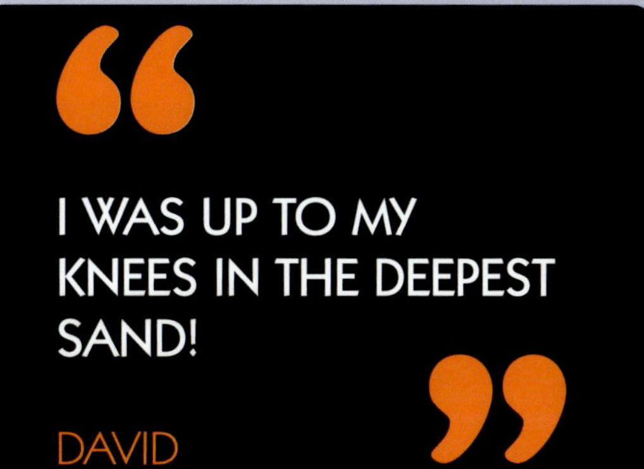

LOSING TOENAILS

David lost three toenails by the end of the marathon. Mark lost all ten toenails by the end of the race! Pressure from their shoes eventually made the nails drop off.

Sand and Friction

Sand and friction can cause the worst damage. When small grains of sand got into David's running shoes, they rubbed against his skin and caused painful blisters.

David wore gaiters to keep the sand out of his shoes. Gaiters are like large "overshoes" made from light, strong nylon.

Earth Science

The Sahara Desert is Not All Sand

Only about 25 per cent of the Sahara Desert is sand and sand dunes. The rest is rocky gravel plains, mountain ranges and lakes.

the Sahara Desert

6 Running with Gravity

Down with **Gravity**

When runners fell over in the *Marathon des Sables*, gravity was the force that made them fall.

During the 245-kilometre marathon, many of the competitors fell over. Runners tripped over rocks and many fell because of extreme tiredness.

RUNNER VERSUS GRAVITY

Tired marathon runners need to use their own energy to resist the pull of gravity.

A runner cools off under a water fountain after running 80 kilometres in one day.

Earth Science

Long, Hot Days!

The heat in the Sahara Desert is so extreme that marathon runners can become very tired from the heat.

Daytime temperatures can reach 50 degrees Celsius. The long, hot days slow down most marathon runners who are not used to the conditions.

(Left) Cambodian girls reading books provided by the Room to Read charity. (Above) Students in front of Room to Read's 2000th library.

Runners Raise Money for Charities

Many runners in the *Marathon des Sables* want to raise money for a charity. David's charity was Room to Read.

Since the year 2000, the Room to Read charity has helped over four million children in nine poor or developing countries, including Nepal, India, Vietnam and South Africa.

The charity does many things, such as:

- builds schools in villages
- establishes libraries for the millions of books donated from other countries
- organises local authors and illustrators to write and illustrate books about their area
- runs education programs especially for girls
- raises money to pay for children to be educated.

Children reading in a library built by the Room to Read charity.

7 Who Won the Marathon?

Everyone **Wins**!

Everyone who finishes the toughest footrace in the world is a winner!

In the 2008 *Marathon des Sables*, David finished the 245-kilometre race in 32 hours, 56 minutes and 23 seconds. Mark finished the race in 35 hours, 1 minute and 41 seconds. Out of 801 runners, David finished in 107th place, and Mark finished in 147th place.

David (right) and Mark Simon after the Marathon des Sables

Social Studies

Marathon des Sables Winners

In the 2010 Marathon des Sables, the men's winner was Mohamad Ahansal from Morocco. He won the 250-kilometre race in 19 hours, 45 minutes and 8 seconds. He has won the race in 1998, 2008, 2009 and 2010. The women's winner was Spanish runner Monica Aguilera Viladomiu, who won the race in 29 hours, 34 minutes and 11 seconds. Mohamad's brother, Lahcen Ahansal, has won the Marathon des Sables ten times – in 1997, and from 1999 to 2007.

Mark with Mohamad Ahansal in 2008

Prizes for Winning?

People don't enter the *Marathon des Sables* for the prize money. They enter the race to:

- challenge themselves
- raise money for a charity, or
- support a team.

The cash prizes for winning vary. They can be between 3000 Euros and 5000 Euros.

EURO

One Euro is worth almost two Australian dollars. That value can change on a daily basis.

Mohamad Ahansal wins the Marathon des Sables *again in 2010!*

Index

Glossary

intake	The amount of something, such as water, that a person needs to put into their body to function properly
masses	Things that have volume and weight
Moroccan	Associated with the country of Morocco, situated in North Africa
motion	Movement
muscle cramps	The pain that is experienced when muscles cannot get rid of their waste products quickly enough
ration (water)	An allowance or amount that must be used
Sahara Desert	A large, hot and dry area that extends across much of North Africa
ultra-marathon	A race that requires extreme fitness and endurance, even more so than in an ordinary marathon